THE NORTH

First published in Great Britain in 2009 by
Young Writers, Remus House, Coltsfoot Drive,
Peterborough, PE2 9JX
Tel (01733) 890066 Fax (01733) 313524
All Rights Reserved

© Copyright Contributors 2009
SB ISBN 978-1-84924-545-6

Foreword

Since Young Writers was established in 1990, our aim has been to promote and encourage written creativity amongst children and young adults. By giving aspiring young authors the chance to be published, Young Writers effectively nurtures the creative talents of the next generation, allowing their confidence and writing ability to grow.

With our latest fun competition, *Mini Sagas*, primary school children nationwide were given the tricky challenge of writing a story with a beginning, middle and an end in just fifty words.

The diverse and imaginative range of entries made the selection process a difficult but enjoyable task with stories chosen on the basis of style, expression, flair and technical skill. A fascinating glimpse into the imaginations of the future, we hope you will agree that this entertaining collection is one that will amuse and inspire the whole family.

Contents

Arnside National School, Arnside
James Reid (10)..1
Cobi Hoare (9) 2
Mike Adair (10)..3
Ashleigh Murphy (10) 4
Joe Till (10)...5
Georgia Beaumont (10)...................................6
William Sewell (9)...7
Aaron Cragg (10)..8
Joshua Smith (10)..9
Anya Shore (9)..10
Abigail Dickson (9) 11
Jack Walker (10) 12
Glen Salter (10) 13
Alessandra Gibson (10)...................................14
Lucy Abbit (10)..15

Buckingham Primary School, Hull
Antonia Stark (11) 16
Connor Gibbs (11) 17
Ellie Willingham (10) 18
Phillipa Johnson (11) 19
Lois Rhodes (11)..20
Rebecca Hubbard (11) 21
Abbey Townend (11) 22
Alisha Smith (10)..23

Chelsea Larney (10) 24
Tye Robertson (11)..25

Cherry Dale Primary School, Cudworth
Elle-Mae Hopkins (9)......................................26
Cassidy Bell (9)..27

Cononley Primary School, Cononley
Megan Rolph (11) 28
Martha Hogg (10) 29
Stacy Black (11) 30
Luke Dyson (11) 31
Theo Hartley (10)..32
Jodie Heaton (11) 33
Sam Birks (11) 34
Bryony Radtke (10)..35
Edward Naylor (10)..36
Megan Hall (11) 37
Ryan McNicholl (11) 38

Highfield Middle School, Prudhoe
David Tyrrell (11)...39
James Watson (11)...40

Longridge CE Primary School, Preston

Jordan Davey (11)............................41
Thomas Windsor (11) 42
Christina Collinson (11)....................43
George Green (11)...........................44
Pippa Beardsley (11)........................45
Henry Scott (11)..............................46
Shannon Coolican (11) 47
Robert Quick (10) 48
Xsara Rainford (11) 49
Heather Holden (11)........................50
Jonathan Shaw (10)..........................51
Laura Langtree (10)..........................52
Sophie Monks (11)...........................53
Melody Golder (10).........................54
Katy Dewison (11)...........................55
Lucy Robinson (11)..........................56
Holly Watson (11) 57
Rhian Kitching (10) 58
Georgina Yates (11) 59
Daniel Andrews (11) 60
Bryony Wood (11)...........................61

Red Lane Primary School, Bolton

Ceejay Smith (10)............................62
Mia Cunningham (10) 63
Lewis Craig (10) 64
Jamie Wright (11) 65
Liam Touch (11)..............................66
Casey Bates (11)..............................67

Bethany Greenwood (10)..................68

Rolls Crescent Primary School, Hulme

Patrice Preddie (10).........................69
Qammar-Ul-Haq Sethi (11)...............70
Zharque Patterson (11) 71
Sigrid-Marion Carbajal (11) 72
Demi-Lee Bridge-Banks (11)............73
Leon Errol Gledhill (11)....................74
Jasmine Johnson (10) 75

Roseberry CP School, Great Ayton

Kieran Husband (11) 76
Benjamin Houldsworth (10)..............77
Daniel Harvey (11) 78
Jessica Bone (10) 79
Robyn Wrigley (10).........................80
Katherine Young (11) 81
Nathan Richardson (10)....................82
William Jackson (11) 83
Jack Swallow (10) 84
Anna Burton (10)............................85
Joe McElvaney (11).........................86
James Horn (11) 87
Georgia Scott (11) 88
Rebekah Adams (11) 89
George Bourne (10) 90
Josh Walton (10)..............................91
Christopher Bone (11) 92
Jessica Edwards (11)........................93

Katie Johnson (10) 94
Patrick Hughes (10) 95
Hannah van der Voet (11) 96
Jack Laskey (11)..............................97
Melissa Storey (10) 98
Verity Charlton (10) 99
Matthew Jewitt (10) 100
Elinor Northey (10)........................101
Rebecca Stokeld (11)......................102
Luke Edwards (9) 103
Hamish Tierney (10).......................104
George Walker (10).........................105
Daniel Houldsworth (10)................106
Beth Hutchinson (11) 107
Matthew Foster (10) 108
Alfie Haydon (10) 109
Adam Wilson (11)...........................110
Joel Hutton (10).............................111
Ashley Healey (10) 112
Emily Sheridan (11) 113
Josh Crombie (11) 114
Marcus Elliott (10) 115
Lucy Fletcher (11) 116
Owen Lyons (10)............................117
Kaitlin Stokeld (11) 118
Dan Hodgson (9) 119
Emma Jane Triptree (10) 120
Tia Ellahi (11) 121
Hannah Tait (10)............................122
Jodie Vaughan (10).........................123
Amy Finch (10) 124

Rebecca Storey (11) 125
Yazdan Qafouri (10).......................126
Joe Thomas (10) 127
Luke Banfield (11) 128
Simon Watson (10) 129
Bronwen Edwards (10) 130
Noah Roberts (11)..........................131
Rachel Harvie (10)..........................132
George Marsden (10) 133

**St Joseph's RC Primary School,
Chorley**
Gabrielle Margerison (10)...............134
Niamh McGuigan (10) 135

**St Raphael's Catholic Primary
School, Millbrook**
Lewis Thompson (11) 136
Connor Penston (11) 137
Jake Chadwick (11) 138
Calum Berry (11)............................139
Nicole Lumley (10).........................140
Sophie Fairhurst (10) 141
Andrew Robinson (11) 142

**Stanhope Barrington School,
Stanhope**
Sam Patterson (9)...........................143
Louise Unsworth (7) 144
Tom Lee (8) 145
Jake Collingwood (7) 146
Adam Young (9)..............................147

Amy Pinel (8)...............................148
Timea Dunnery (8)..........................149
Mollie Adams (8)...........................150
Georgia Wright (9).........................151
Sophie Bowman (9)..........................152
Olivia Parkin (8)..........................153
George Haynes (8)..........................154
Thomas Williams (8)........................155
Ellie Gardiner (9).........................156
Lauren Lee (8).............................157
William Nattrass (9).......................158
Jason Humble (8)...........................159
Morgan Allen (8)...........................160
Ryan Mackay (7)............................161
Pippa Smith (8)............................162

Stanley Crook Primary School, Stanley Crook

Arran Stobart (9)..........................163
Rebecca Moore (9)..........................164
Georgia O'Connor (9).......................165
Nathan Hodgson (9).........................166
Liam Clark (9).............................167
Lewis Clark (9)............................168
Jak Hope (8)...............................169
Christopher Callaway (8)...................170
Emma Macdonald (8).........................171
Shania Klijn (9)...........................172
Reece Liddle (9)...........................173
Ryan Robson (8)............................174
Ben Robison (8)............................175

Reese Brown (8)............................176
Arron Stores (8)...........................177
Chloe Shevels (7)..........................178
Elise Moore (8)............................179
Louis Gilligan (8).........................180
Abby Clark (7).............................181
Liam Walsh (8).............................182

Startforth Morritt Primary School, Barnard Castle

Kennedy Zipfel (9).........................183
Nathan Kirby (10)..........................184
Alice Peat (9).............................185
Lenny McLennan (10)........................186
Katie Knox (10)............................187
Sasha Wilkes (9)...........................188
James Barber (9)...........................189
Jasmine Banes (9)..........................190
Peter Atkinson (10)........................191
Britty Farren (10).........................192
Victoria Hanley (9)........................193
Evelyn Ridgway (9).........................194
Owen Lewis (10)............................195
Michaela Leslie (10).......................196
Kane Wynn-Jones (10).......................197

Thorpepark Primary School, Hull

Adam Rumkee (11)...........................198
Luke Phillips (10).........................199
Harry King (10)............................200

Warmingham CE Primary School, Warmingham

Thomas Howard (9)....................................201
Ben Nelson (11) 202
Mitch Crank (11) 203
Ollie Holmes (9).....................................204
Yasmin Harrison (8)..................................205
Kate Olbrich (9).....................................206
Joshua Bebbington (8) 207

The Mini Sagas

Late Out

The blacked out sky made the scattered stars
gleam as the little hideout stood out like a
lighthouse circulating a wide bay. I tried the
door but it was locked, like a python guarding its
territory. I got a rock and launched it at the lock
and astonishingly it opened.

James Reid (10)
Arnside National School, Arnside

The Dark Hillbilly Farm

I was stuck on a large hillbilly farm, I could hear a hillbilly cow. Then I found blue hillbilly houses nearby. I went inside one, it had nothing inside but dust and some small ants, but then the door smashed down to the ground …

Cobi Hoare (9)
Arnside National School, Arnside

Ducky Ghouls

Ducky was at the intersection of Conshaun Chorale, cornered by ghostly ghouls getting him with beams and lasers. He ran to the telephone box to ring the police. Two minutes later they were in on it but they had no ghostly ray, so they chased the ghouls away with sticks.

Mike Adair (10)

Arnside National School, Arnside

A Day In The Life
Of A Georgian Mistress

I woke up in silk sheets in a bed chamber. My maiden suddenly came in and started helping me get dressed. When I was ready to go downstairs I was wearing a bleach blonde wig with fruit in it and a big layered brown dress with cream lace ribbons.

Ashleigh Murphy (10)
Arnside National School, Arnside

4

Alone In The Forest

Suddenly there were trees scattered around. A
house caught my eye. I heard a screaming noise, I
thought my heart would come out of my mouth.
So I ran as quickly as I could but I fell over a stick.
I thought I was going to die … I said goodbye.

Joe Till (10)
Arnside National School, Arnside

Ghostly Goings-On

The drawbridge dropped and crashed to the
sandy ground. I wandered inside and met a
spooky looking ghost. The ghost was transparent
and hadn't seen me, so I crept quietly into the
castle and a wondrous sight met my eyes. The
castle was filled with partying, friendly ghosts
messing around.

Georgia Beaumont (10)
Arnside National School, Arnside

Never-Ending Art

As I looked down the never-ending corridor
the high walls seemed to close in on me like a
car crusher. Realising the large walls were going
to crush me, I tried even harder to find an exit.
I removed a long painting to find a large door,
'There … phew!'

William Sewell (9)
Arnside National School, Arnside

Ghostly Goings-On

One misty night, down a thin alley stood a little, lopsided, creepy, haunted house. In the house the window opened slowly and a little black shadow moved cautiously. The shadow jumped out of the little window, then I knew the person was surprisingly skinny. The room then closed up slowly …

Aaron Cragg (10)
Arnside National School, Arnside

You're Dead

The rusty oil barrels were scattered roughly around the old, crumpled hotel. Suddenly a gruesome army of dark figures limped out from the spiky reeds, then the black knight emerged from the shadows and he spoke in a deep voice. He said, 'I challenge you – single combat battle to death.'

Joshua Smith (10)
Arnside National School, Arnside

Alone

I awoke with a start, trees surrounded me like men with piercing eyes. I knew that I was lost, the moon had expanded, it looked as if it was going to lurch out and devour me. My heart was beating so fast, I couldn't breathe, I started running really fast.

Anya Shore (9)

Arnside National School, Arnside

Night At The Museum 500

The unwelcoming museum felt like it was
creeping in on me … Suddenly I heard the door
lock, 'I'm trapped!' I screamed. But slowly the
exhibits started to move and crowd me into the
dark corner … Just then, I had an amazing idea,
I'd leap out of the nearest open window …

Abigail Dickson (9)
Arnside National School, Arnside

Alone

I was locked in an old wooden shed with no food, I was starving. I was hoping someone would unlock the door and let me out but I knew I would never get out. I fell asleep but after a while I suddenly woke up and the door was open!

Jack Walker (10)
Arnside National School, Arnside

Lost

In the never-ending hall of mirrors the lights went out, little Jimmy Shoemaker was lost. As he ran through the endless corridor he thought he saw a figure of a tall dark man, but it was just a mere reflection of himself, how would he ever escape?

Glen Salter (10)

Arnside National School, Arnside

Shakespeare's Idea

One day, at Mystical Moors Waterfall,
Shakespeare sat down on the dark, wet stone,
with the cool breeze blowing down on his face.
He didn't know what to do to amuse himself.
But then William Shakespeare had the superbly
brilliant idea that would change his whole life
forever and ever ...

Alessandra Gibson (10)
Arnside National School, Arnside

14

Ghostly Goings-On

The creepy cottage creaked as I slowly walked through the wooden corridor. The breeze rattled the windows, I searched, frantically tapping on the brick walls. I dropped to the floor and found a trapdoor. It suddenly burst open, I fell through and found myself looking at a scary ghost!

Lucy Abbit (10)
Arnside National School, Arnside

A New School

Starting a new school, in a different uniform, was difficult for Amber, especially as the other children looked so mean. As she entered through the gates she saw many aggressive-looking children. Some children walked up and surrounded her. Fortunately a teacher spotted them. She was safe … for a while.

Antonia Stark (11)
Buckingham Primary School, Hull

The Mist!

Staring into the thickening mist I remembered 9,000 souls had been lost on this journey to Hell. Was I next? A pain burned through my chest, *what's happening?* I drank the witch's potion and my chest eased, but not for long … Goodbye to this cruel, heartless world – time for Hell!

Connor Gibbs (11)
Buckingham Primary School, Hull

Victorian Times?

As I stared into my grandma's old mirror, a peculiar feeling enveloped me. I was looking at people in strange Victorian-type clothing. What did it mean? I stood there perplexed as a voice brought me back to reality. 'Do you like my old Victorian mirror?' asked Grandma.

Ellie Willingham (10)
Buckingham Primary School, Hull

Mirror

Rose glanced in the mirror and remembered
what had happened before. 'Will it happen again?'
As she said that, everything went hazy. Lots of
people were standing around her. 'Is she OK?'
asked one person. Suddenly Rose jumped out of
the dentist's chair, *never again,* she thought.

Phillipa Johnson (11)
Buckingham Primary School, Hull

Jason And The Golden Fleece

It was a dark night and Jason was sitting on his fleece. He was all alone, hungry and feeling useless. He had no family or friends in New York and although he was a millionaire he felt like a tramp. What use was a golden fleece to him now?

Lois Rhodes (11)
Buckingham Primary School, Hull

Lost In Time

Lucy stared around in fright. There it was, standing tall, an old Victorian house. It started to shake with the wind, the creaking was terrifying. The wind battered the walls. Would it crash? In a matter of minutes it fell. The floor vibrated and both Lucy and the house disappeared.

Rebecca Hubbard (11)
Buckingham Primary School, Hull

Terror Drop

The sun was beating down and there were no clouds in the sky, but my heart was pounding. I trembled as it shot downwards, everyone screaming. Finally the carriage reached the end of the drop, but then I saw it, another steep drop, and I was advancing towards it quickly …

Abbey Townend (11)
Buckingham Primary School, Hull

Alone?

Accepting the dare, I entered the creepy, old home. The air was thick with dust and a strange musty smell. A creak startled me. Then a door slammed shut. I'd had enough. Trembling, I dashed with fear out of the house to the laughter of my giggling friends.

Alisha Smith (10)
Buckingham Primary School, Hull

The Dream

I kept running but was it still chasing me?
Suddenly I realised it was a dead end. It came
round the corner, I was trapped. It came closer
and closer. It got out its claws and hissed at me.
Then I woke up. It was just a dream. *Phew!*

Chelsea Larney (10)
Buckingham Primary School, Hull

Perseus And The Cyclops

Perseus volunteered to kill the deadly beast inside
the maze. He entered the maze, armed only with
his short sword. He listened. Soon he could hear
the snorting of its breath even though his own
heart pounded loudly in his chest. It was time for
battle. To do … or die.

Tye Robertson (11)
Buckingham Primary School, Hull

The Death Walk

I walked down the dark, dismal, gloomy alley. I saw a red, bubbling blob on the dry, grey ground. Was it blood? I didn't know. I walked on and on, feeling very frightened and terrified. After following the blobs to the end of the alley I saw, to my surprise ...

Elle-Mae Hopkins (9)
Cherry Dale Primary School, Cudworth

Legend

Theseus was King Aegeus' son. He wanted to go to Crete to kill King Minos' Minotaur. Theseus explained to his father that if he killed the Minotaur he would change his ship's sail from black to white on his return. This he forgot, and his father hung himself. How sad.

Cassidy Bell (9)
Cherry Dale Primary School, Cudworth

A Black Unicorn

Saltwater poured into my mouth, burning my throat. The stormy grey waves threw me around mercilessly. Darkness threatened to close in on me. I saw a dark, blurry shape. Then everything went black … I woke up at the beach. A beautiful black unicorn was flying away into the distance …

Megan Rolph (11)

Cononley Primary School, Cononley

The Little Toaster

Timmy was a toaster. His family moved out. He was alone. He went to find them and got lost in the Forest of Doom. Then Timmy met a light bulb called Bob. They became friends and escaped. Timmy had made a new friend and didn't need his family anymore.

Martha Hogg (10)
Cononley Primary School, Cononley

Was It A Dream?

I had chains around my ankles … a man with a thick beard came around the corner, 'Here's your meal,' he said. He gave me one crust of bread. He walked away, I was too scared to eat it. I woke up in bed but had chain marks around my ankles …

Stacy Black (11)
Cononley Primary School, Cononley

The King Of The Skies

I flew around Egypt, soaring over the sand and above the pyramids, I flew over Cairo and subtly landed in a deserted alleyway. I thought no one had seen me. I retracted my wings and was about to go out. Suddenly ten jackal-headed warriors erupted out of the buildings …

Luke Dyson (11)
Cononley Primary School, Cononley

Freddy The Frog

Freddy was a frog. He liked to swim and dive.
One day Freddy dived down to the bottom of the
lake. Freddy found a jewel at the bottom of the
lake. Freddy found a poster saying that the jewel
was someone else's. Freddy returned the jewel
and got a reward.

Theo Hartley (10)
Cononley Primary School, Cononley

A Mystery

I was by myself in school at night-time. Someone once died on the floor in the toilets. *Who did that? Oh no! I can hear someone coming towards me.* Quietly I ran into a toilet, someone looked in the toilet I was in, I was too scared to move …

Jodie Heaton (11)
Cononley Primary School, Cononley

The Haribo Teddy

Once upon a time there was a green Haribo teddy who was chased by a hungry child. The Haribo teddy ran and ran as fast as he could. He tried to run away from the child so he ran to his mum and his mum chased and scared the child.

Sam Birks (11)
Cononley Primary School, Cononley

Was It Real?

I woke up, I was in the middle of a forest, I could hardly see, the only thing helping me was the moonlight. I suddenly realised I was tangled up in the tree roots. I struggled but it was no use, they started to scratch me. Suddenly I awoke ...

Bryony Radtke (10)
Cononley Primary School, Cononley

Off To Table Tennis

Off I went to table tennis on a Thursday night. It was really dark and I got lost; I didn't know where I was. There it was, a ghost sat there, but then it chased me. I ran and found my table tennis racket and everyone killed it.

Edward Naylor (10)
Cononley Primary School, Cononley

36

The Gigantic Wolves

One day three wolves were sent away from home by their mother, Pipa Pig, who said they were too big to stay. So they made their own houses, one was paper, one was clothes and one was speakers that blasted out loud rock music. They lived there forever.

Megan Hall (11)
Cononley Primary School, Cononley

Beginning Of The End

Three people have died. We have been trying to
find the suspect of the crime, they all had dinner
at the New Inn. We go there, question them
about it. They say they have no chef. We go into
the kitchen and see a fly in the food …

Ryan McNicholl (11)
Cononley Primary School, Cononley

Crash, Bang Wallop

I walked in, hoping for a hello. 'Where is everyone?' I said. The lights went off … *bang, bang, bang*. The lights went on. I found I got hit with a bunch of tomatoes, bananas and a huge amount of chocolate. I replied, 'Thanks … for the chocolate.'

David Tyrrell (11)
Highfield Middle School, Prudhoe

What Is It?

I walked into the dark forest, shrieks were coming from every corner. What was happening? But there was no pain, then there was somebody speaking over them. It all became silent. I ran to see what was happening. I got caught. Why did I have to go to school?

James Watson (11)
Highfield Middle School, Prudhoe

The Mysterious

There was a boy called John, he went to his
bedroom. The light flickered on and off, he
jumped off the bed and saw a body disappear.
He ran down the stairs. There was a bang in the
basement. He went down and the door locked on
its own …

Jordan Davey (11)
Longridge CE Primary School, Preston

Night Of The Walking Bob

One night in a dark graveyard Bill was visiting his friend Bob's grave. Suddenly the ground shuddered and Bob's grave split open and Bob came out. Bill screamed as Bob pounced on him and ate his brain. He then started his quest to find his killer.

Thomas Windsor (11)
Longridge CE Primary School, Preston

42

The Evil Teacher

The evil teacher was called Mrs Cross, she made Class 6 do ten pieces of homework and forced them to eat torturing school dinners, but Christina was there to save the school. She killed her by throwing rubbers at her so the evil teacher was killed, or was she?

Christina Collinson (11)
Longridge CE Primary School, Preston

Lost In A Desert!

The sun was hot. I could not move, speak or blink. I was so thirsty, I would have done anything just for a tiny sip of water, but all I could see was sand everywhere. Then suddenly some people started to run at me from nowhere!

George Green (11)
Longridge CE Primary School, Preston

The Commercial

I was on my way to the TV studio, when I got lost. I was in … a lab! 'Ahh, cute mice. *Sssssnake!*' I ran through the door. I was at the studio. It was all part of the commercial, advertising Satnav. I never knew advertising could be so surprising!

Pippa Beardsley (11)
Longridge CE Primary School, Preston

Five In One

It was Friday, takeaway night. Matthew went to Five In One, it was dark, there were strange noises coming from the kitchen. Suddenly a man with a pizza came close, he put his hand on Matthew's shoulder and said: 'You are our 1,000th customer.' And his camera went *click!*

Henry Scott (11)
Longridge CE Primary School, Preston

Shower Problem!

Norbert the ogre woke up one morning and found he had lost his shower cap. He went for a shower without his shower cap and used his bright pink undies instead. Then he noticed his undies were wet so he used Baby Ogre's nappy. That sorted the problem!

Shannon Coolican (11)
Longridge CE Primary School, Preston

The Krakon

Simon was on his ship in the middle of nowhere.
He had been travelling for just over 2 hours and
there was no food left on the ship. The crew
were trying to eat each other. Suddenly the boat
began to rock. There it was, the fierce kraken.

Robert Quick (10)
Longridge CE Primary School, Preston

Orange!

I got a goldfish today but it's orange. Mum said goldfish, not orangefish. I wanted a goldfish but Mum said there's no such thing. She said they only come in orange. That's not fair though, fine, let's go get him some friends called Billybob and Jingles.

Xsara Rainford (11)
Longridge CE Primary School, Preston

Splat!

One day a yellow bird flew to my window,
it came too close and went *splat!* Then a fox
climbed on top of my dustbin but it fell in and
went *splat!* Then next door's cat came on my
roof, fell down the chimney and went ... *splat!*

Heather Holden (11)
Longridge CE Primary School, Preston

Humpty Dumpty

Humpty Dumpty sat on a wall drinking some Oasis, he got attacked by ninjas. He started fighting back. He punched one in the face and kicked one in the shin. Humpty Dumpty sat on a wall and had a great fall.

Jonathan Shaw (10)
Longridge CE Primary School, Preston

Deadly Woods

I was standing in the woods, looking for movement. I heard a dramatic sound from the water. A pair of eyes appeared from above the water. The thing stood up and started charging towards me. I opened my eyes and realised I was in the park, daydreaming.

Laura Langtree (10)
Longridge CE Primary School, Preston

Breathless

Breathless, I ran up the stairs, two at a time. I turned, wondering who it was following me. I could still hear footsteps behind me … I carried on running. I tripped and fell, I listened, they'd finally stopped. What had happened? Where had they gone? It was a complete mystery …

Sophie Monks (11)
Longridge CE Primary School, Preston

Untitled

One day some people moved in next door, the house looked black and dark. I went inside to see what all the noise was, and there it was – the ghost, it was whizzing about, up and down. It came closer and closer, then it stopped right in front of me …

Melody Golder (10)
Longridge CE Primary School, Preston

54

In The Future

I wake up, where am I? The last thing I remember is getting some frozen chips from the freezer. Hey, I must be in the future. I can pretend my name is Super Katy (my name is Katy).
'Katy, Coronation Street's on!' Oh, I'm not in the future after all.

Katy Dewison (11)
Longridge CE Primary School, Preston

55

Runaway Tortoise

Trevor is my tortoise, one day he ran, well crawled, away. He climbed up out of his cage and made his escape through the kitchen. He caught a lift in my remote control car and went through the front door, down the road, round the corner, past the shopping centre …

Lucy Robinson (11)
Longridge CE Primary School, Preston

Smile Catcher

The smile catcher was a terrifying man with eyes
like golf balls that stuck far out of his ugly face,
and he looked like a frog. He worked at night
and caught smiles by making people feel upset,
sad and lonely. I was terrified when he walked
towards me!

Holly Watson (11)
Longridge CE Primary School, Preston

The Man In The Mirror

Sam went into the basement of his new gloomy
house, he looked into the mirror hanging on the
wall but … it wasn't his own reflection looking
back. Suddenly the lights turned off. Sam jumped,
but didn't make noise. The lights turned back on.
Sam's reflection was back in the mirror.

Rhian Kitching (10)
Longridge CE Primary School, Preston

No One Around!

It's my birthday today, I am 11. All my family
have gone shopping, I'm all on my own. A big
bang makes me shiver with fear, it's coming from
behind me. I quickly turn around, silly me, it's my
cat playing with its toy mouse. 'Come on Tickles.'

Georgina Yates (11)
Longridge CE Primary School, Preston

The Devil's Surprise

As the Devil came to eat the human banquet, in front of him he heard a knock on the door. With all his anger he flame grilled his meal. 'Who's that at this time of night? Guard bring whoever knocked to me. They'll have a surprise! *Ha ha ha!*'

Daniel Andrews (11)
Longridge CE Primary School, Preston

My Adventure Holiday

As I walked nervously up the high stairs to
the high ropes I tripped over my evil enemy,
Charlotte. I cut my knee but I didn't tell anyone,
so I let it bleed, but then the teacher saw it and
took me to the nurse outside the high ropes.

Bryony Wood (11)
Longridge CE Primary School, Preston

The Fortune Teller

The Minotaur walked into the cave, looking
for somewhere to sleep. The Minotaur found
a secret room with a fortune teller in it. The
fortune teller told him he would be tortured by
villagers. 'I don't believe you,' he said.
He heard voices, 'He's over there, attack!'
'Help me … !'

Ceejay Smith (10)
Red Lane Primary School, Bolton

62

Slippery Bridge

The sun shining on the water, the wildlife waving
in the wind, the frogs splashed water and
sprinkled drops on me. I walked on the bridge.
Suddenly I slipped on the bridge over the water.
Fortunately a couple helped me up and took me
home.

Mia Cunningham (10)
Red Lane Primary School, Bolton

The Cub That Tried To Escape

The zoo was quiet, all the people had gone. The cage quietly opened and the animals escaped calmly but the lions disappeared and all there was left was a cub. He was scared because he was going to the exit of the zoo and an alarm was going off.

Lewis Craig (10)

Red Lane Primary School, Bolton

64

The Great Escape

The visitors disappeared. It was dark and silent, cage doors opened. Creatures emerged out and stretched but the little lion cub headed for the exit gate of the zoo, or should I say danger zone. When the lion cub hit the alarm button by mistake …

Jamie Wright (11)
Red Lane Primary School, Bolton

Life In A Pond

The baby tadpole wandered the pond feeling ill.
All the other frogs looked different to him. He
went to see a doctor who said, 'You're just late in
evolving.'
The next day the tadpole had changed colour and
he had lost his tail. He was finally a frog.

Liam Touch (11)
Red Lane Primary School, Bolton

Horses And Me

The noise of the horses galloping, people gathered round their stables. You could hear the sound of people shouting and horses banging their stable doors. The atmosphere was crazy. As I tried on hats I couldn't find one which fit me …

Casey Bates (11)
Red Lane Primary School, Bolton

Dust At Dawn

The night guard was asleep. Statues were slowly moving, escaping out of the museum. He heard a *bang!* He crept out to discover the animals gone, except one, Gilbert. He told him they were heading for the park, but at dawn he'd turn to dust. It was almost dawn …

Bethany Greenwood (10)

Red Lane Primary School, Bolton

In The Dangerous Woods

It was a dark, scary night in the woods where mean and nasty animals rest. On that very same night a little girl came into the woods because she was lost and she didn't know where to go, unexpectedly she heard a snap of a twig. *Grrr!* 'Help!'

Patrice Preddie (10)
Rolls Crescent Primary School, Hulme

Downhearted

'Happy birthday Zoey,' yell her friends, family and colleagues at the top of their voices. Zoey blows out the candle and smiles. But, deep down, hidden beneath that smile is actually sadness. She doesn't find joy in celebrating her one year closer to oblivion. In fact, she simply resents it.

Qammar-Ul-Haq Sethi (11)
Rolls Crescent Primary School, Hulme

Alone In The House

The abandoned house is empty. *Thought this was meant to be a party, where is everyone? I'm going now, I'm supposed to be at home.* I decided to come here and look, no one is even here.

'Surprise!'

'Weren't you all at my mum's? Doesn't matter.'

Zharque Patterson (11)
Rolls Crescent Primary School, Hulme

71

Blood On The Floor

It was a dark night in the forest and blood stained the floor. Tyson and Amy looked at the fox. It had a big bite out of it. 'What could've happened?' asked Amy.

'I don't know,' replied Tyson.

Little did they know that they were about to find out what …

Sigrid-Marion Carbajal (11)

Rolls Crescent Primary School, Hulme

The Superhero

The superhero is small but strong, he is a handsome boy. Once a little girl was stuck in a building with a bomb and the superhero saved her. People were watching and congratulated him. Then they celebrated, because he was very small and young and it was his first time.

Demi-Lee Bridge-Banks (11)

Rolls Crescent Primary School, Hulme

The Dare Game

I wish I hadn't agreed to play the stupid game. Dale only dared me to go into the forest because he was too afraid. As I walked into the dark, deserted forest Dale ran off. 'Wimp!' I shouted. A sound from behind startled me, I spun round to see … *Aarrgghh* …

Leon Errol Gledhill (11)
Rolls Crescent Primary School, Hulme

74

Left Behind In The Rapture

It was a summer-sweet day. Everyone around was
talking, when suddenly they noticed people had
disappeared. The only thing left behind was their
clothes. Everyone was frightened. They noticed
that all the saints and good, godly people were
gone. It was the rapture! What would they do
here now?

Jasmine Johnson (10)
Rolls Crescent Primary School, Hulme

The Crocodile

He was rowing his little boat down a calm river with his dog sat next to him. He'd been rowing for about half an hour, when out of the water the boy saw a giant, ferocious crocodile about 20 yards away. It came closer and closer and then ... 'Argh!'

Kieran Husband (11)
Roseberry CP School, Great Ayton

The Accident

The wizard got out his wand. He took a deep
breath. 'Abracadabra,' he cried. There was a flash
of green light. Trees toppled like matchsticks.
Bushes were blown away. A cold grey mist
descended on the forest. As the mist settled,
there was not a living thing in sight.

Benjamin Houldsworth (10)
Roseberry CP School, Great Ayton

The Jester's Mistake

There was once a jester who performed for King
Arthur. However he could not make him laugh,
although he had tried for many years.
One day, the jester thought of a joke but the King
didn't find it funny, although he chuckled as he cut
off his head!

Daniel Harvey (11)
Roseberry CP School, Great Ayton

Emergency

I receive a phone call. 'Mum's broken her arm.' I
study the map. Which way do I go, left, the long
way round or right, the short way through the
ford? Right! Too much water! Turn round and go
the long way. 'Sorry I'm late. Let's go to casualty.'

Jessica Bone (10)
Roseberry CP School, Great Ayton

Blocked

There's a house nobody goes in. It's a big, black house. Would you go in? Two years ago a woman lived there all cheerful. One day the woman vanished. No sign. Nothing. Just silence. The house has never been touched again. It's now locked. All gone.

Robyn Wrigley (10)
Roseberry CP School, Great Ayton

Doughnuts!

'Ha, ha, ha!' cackled the mad scientist. 'Sing my
darlings, sing!'
'We are walking doughnuts here to take over the
world!' sang the doughnuts.
'Left, right, left, right!' yelled Sergeant Jam. 'Halt!'
'Go my darlings, go and destroy all the sweet
shops!' ordered the scientist.
'Yes Sir!' chanted the doughnuts.

Katherine Young (11)
Roseberry CP School, Great Ayton

The Living Blob

The mad scientist was sprinting round the lab,
trying to find a formula. Accidentally he knocked
a poison over by mistake, but he left it for now.
Then it started to grow massive. After that he
turned round and saw an enormous blob. Next
the blob ate the mad scientist!

Nathan Richardson (10)
Roseberry CP School, Great Ayton

The Haunted Biscuit Tin

The lid was off and I was being tortured by the delicious cookies. It was like they were hypnotising me. That's it, I couldn't bear it any longer. When no one was looking I went for one. When my hand reached the tin everything went silent, everything was pitch-black.

William Jackson (11)
Roseberry CP School, Great Ayton

The Witch And The Spider

In New York there was a witch creeping around in the dead of night, when suddenly a giant spider crept out from behind a tree and dived at her. She dodged. 'Alacazim!' she shouted. She thought that she killed the spider but she actually turned the whole town into frogs!

Jack Swallow (10)
Roseberry CP School, Great Ayton

Scared

Step, step, step, it was as quiet as a vacuum.
'Where am I? Is anybody there?' I thought, *am I all alone?*
But then I heard, a voice saying, 'In the cupboard, in the cupboard.' I opened the cupboard, what a terrible sight, a creature; slimy, dark at sight!

Anna Burton (10)
Roseberry CP School, Great Ayton

85

The Sloth

The sloth crawled along the branch, moving at the pace of a snail. Just then the roar of a mountain lion struck fear into its very bones. The terrified sloth let go in shock and fell helplessly to the ground. Suddenly the imposing figure of the lion appeared towering above.

Joe McElvaney (11)
Roseberry CP School, Great Ayton

The Alien Intruders

There was a strange colour in the sky, bouncing like a kangaroo. It seemed to be coming down to Earth. Suddenly a big thump shook the ground. A blue, circular ship was balancing on the grass. The door opened!

James Horn (11)
Roseberry CP School, Great Ayton

Crazy Cave

I tiptoed to the opening of a dark cave. Stepping into its giant mouth was terrifying. Even my heart was pounding with fear. As I chased round and round the crazy bends, looking all around me, I realised I was lost! All I'd wanted was my bouncy ball back.

Georgia Scott (11)
Roseberry CP School, Great Ayton

My Eyes

A week after Sara's eye transplant, she was walking through the dark woods. Suddenly she saw a man with gleaming white skin against his black clothes. In his face were two holes as big as caverns where his eyes should have been. All he said was, 'Give me my eyes!'

Rebekah Adams (11)
Roseberry CP School, Great Ayton

The Haunted Mansion

There's a mansion at the top of the hill, my
grandpa says no one has been there for a century.
One frosty night I crept through the back gate
and ran to the mansion. To my horror a ghastly
figure was waiting for me … 'I've been expecting
you Tommy!'

George Bourne (10)
Roseberry CP School, Great Ayton

The Footsteps

Alex heard a noise coming from his bedroom.
It sounded like footsteps, but Mum and Dad
said that they had gone out shopping. Alex went
upstairs. He approached his bedroom and opened
the door. It was pitch-black, but he went in. He
opened the curtains. 'Surprise!'

Josh Walton (10)
Roseberry CP School, Great Ayton

House Horrors

It was spooky as I walked along the dreaded path up to the mysterious house where people never come back out. The door creaked open, I peered in. 'Is there anyone there?' No reply. I slipped inside, then suddenly out of the corner of the room there appeared a ...

Christopher Bone (11)
Roseberry CP School, Great Ayton

The Legend Of The Black Viper

'Right lads, once we're inside the cave we must be very careful of the three-headed dragon-snake, the black viper who guards the precious black diamond. To receive the diamond we must slay the venomous, fire-breathing black viper. There he is lads, shoot and kill, shoot and kill.'

Jessica Edwards (11)
Roseberry CP School, Great Ayton

The Magic Spell!

I'd been working all day. What could I do? It
happened. You may think, *what did she do?* Well,
when you're trying to read and work, it can go
wrong. I must have put in too much bicarbonate
for it to fizz so much. The clearing up took ages.

Katie Johnson (10)
Roseberry CP School, Great Ayton

It

I was strolling down the walkway when I saw it. It had two glowing eyes and four hairy legs. It was running towards me! I crouched down. I closed my eyes, waiting for the inevitable. It came close to my face! Then it licked me. It was my dog Bruno!

Patrick Hughes (10)
Roseberry CP School, Great Ayton

Pitch-Black

It was pitch-black. It felt like the world was spinning. I could hear whispering and laughing. I could feel someone pushing me. I bumped my head. I gently fingered the wall. I pushed something. Something was lifted off my head. 'Surprise!' It was the best birthday surprise.

Hannah van der Voet (11)
Roseberry CP School, Great Ayton

The Alien

It was pitch-black. Jeremy got out of bed to go and get a drink. As he was going downstairs an eerie blue light appeared in the kitchen. Then he heard footsteps coming towards him. Jeremy looked towards the kitchen and screamed!

Jack Laskey (11)
Roseberry CP School, Great Ayton

The Witch's Brew

Boom! Bang! Pop! went the witch's cauldron,
'Ready? Here, drink it!' cackled the witch.
'Argh! What have you done to me? I'm all slimy,'
gulped Ben. There was no reply. Then he heard
the door lock. Poor Ben was never to be seen
again!

Melissa Storey (10)
Roseberry CP School, Great Ayton

98

Talking Doughnuts

The sun was beating down on me as I looked inside the old bakery shop. 'Hey Lucas, don't just stand there, eat me!'

'Who's there?' I said, 'and how do you know my name?'

'Look in the window.'

'Muuuum!'

'What is it?'

'Talking doughnuts!'

'You're right, they do look tasty!'

Verity Charlton (10)
Roseberry CP School, Great Ayton

The Haunted House

Ben crept through the haunted house, looking in
every room. Sneaking, sneaking up the stairs, he
reached the top and pushed open the door. In
front of him was a crowd of moaning zombies!
He rushed down the stairs, collided with another
zombie and was never ever seen again!

Matthew Jewitt (10)
Roseberry CP School, Great Ayton

The Golden Flute

The sun blazed. Lola slumped down onto the
rock. She had scaled Aphrodite's Rock in search
of the golden flute. The more she thought
the more she could imagine it captured in the
rock. Lola dozed off. She sprang up! Some rock
crumbled away. Something gold glittered. Could
it be?

Elinor Northey (10)
Roseberry CP School, Great Ayton

Camping Creeps

'I hate camping,' I said to my parents.
'We're going home tomorrow,' said Mum.
'Good!' I replied grumpily. That night I was woken
by a rattle. I peeped out nervously. Someone
was there with a knife. I tried to scream but my
mouth was dry.
'Cake?' asked Dad!

Rebecca Stokeld (11)
Roseberry CP School, Great Ayton

Alien Crash

One day, in a galaxy far, far, far away lived
some aliens who had a spaceship. Suddenly the
spaceship's engine stopped, they were falling
through space at 1,000 miles an hour. They hit the
atmosphere and crashed on to a lonely planet, but
where were they? Nobody knows.

Luke Edwards (9)
Roseberry CP School, Great Ayton

Untitled

We had entered the middle of the swamp. There was silence everywhere. Then suddenly, out of a dark stream, came a gigantic, slimy swamp monster. We started to run. 'Help!' we screamed. The swamp monster had caught my leg. I struggled, there was no escape.

Hamish Tierney (10)
Roseberry CP School, Great Ayton

The Evil Omen

The evil omen strolls through the dark, dingy streets, unseen, unheard, no scent. But then suddenly a scream pierces the sky, the omen has struck, she shall be cursed. The omen wanders through the dark midnight sky. Hey! He's coming this way, but don't stick around, run for your *life!*

George Walker (10)
Roseberry CP School, Great Ayton

The Lonely Wizard

Gaddolf was ancient and very lonely. He was trying desperately to make some pictures come alive with his wand. So far he hadn't got anywhere with the picture of his mum. 'Alivio,' he muttered, pointing his wand at the picture. Nothing happened. 'Alivo!' he shouted. *Bang!* What had happened … ?

Daniel Houldsworth (10)
Roseberry CP School, Great Ayton

Jack And Gill

One day, a boy and girl were climbing a very tall and steep hill. They were sent up the hill on an errand. *Boom! Boom! Boom!* The boy had tripped and fell down the hill, and after that, the girl came rolling after!

Beth Hutchinson (11)
Roseberry CP School, Great Ayton

Untitled

I was sitting outside happily when suddenly a bright light came out the sky. It looked like an alien spaceship. I stopped, I said to myself, 'It can't be an alien spaceship.' It was! It landed. The alien came out with a gun, but I didn't know what to do.

Matthew Foster (10)
Roseberry CP School, Great Ayton

Lost

Alex and Sophie walked down the endless path, not knowing where they were going. They had walked for months on this grey, dusty path. Alex turned, there was a rusty noise. It must have been the man-eating worm but then appeared … a mouse!

Alfie Haydon (10)
Roseberry CP School, Great Ayton

The Cascading TV

I turned on the TV. Suddenly blood cascaded out. 'Mum, the TV's bleeding!' I screamed. A girl scrambled out. She started waddling around the room mindlessly. 'Argh!' She bit me. My vision blurred. Blood started gushing out of my hand. 'Brains!' I chanted. 'I'm a zombie!' I realised.

Adam Wilson (11)
Roseberry CP School, Great Ayton

Victory

The English soldiers burst into the room in a
stampede. They were looking for Adolf Hitler,
the German leader. But all they found was a stiff,
bloody corpse on his desk. 'It's Hitler,' someone
shouted, 'and he's killed himself!'
'Are you sure?' asked the soldiers.
'Positive.'

Joel Hutton (10)
Roseberry CP School, Great Ayton

The Mystery Bang

The tiger stalked through the jungle looking for some water. The lake in the jungle had dried up for it was summer and it had been scorching hot the day before. Today it was cool and calm in the heart of the jungle. Then he heard the sound of guns.

Ashley Healey (10)
Roseberry CP School, Great Ayton

The Battle Of Marston Moor 1644

The waterfall came from the sky while electricity
darted between clouds and the drum roll
sounded. 'God is with us,' were the cries from
one side and, 'God and King,' was another. The
Royalists were horrified. The hill seemed to be
falling on top of them. The war was won.

Emily Sheridan (11)
Roseberry CP School, Great Ayton

Untitled

1940, German U-boats were crossing the dreaded Bermuda Triangle. The captain felt a small tremor, suddenly a scream, as a huge eye peered in. 'The Kracken!' yelled one of the engineers. But before they could fire the torpedoes a tentacle grabbed the sub and dragged it into its gargantuan mouth ...

Josh Crombie (11)
Roseberry CP School, Great Ayton

Stranded

I was alone, on an island. I was thinking, *why don't I go exploring, I've got to do something here.* I put my coat and shoes on, and off I went. *Bang!* Blood was pouring out of me. Then it was pitch-black.

Marcus Elliott (10)
Roseberry CP School, Great Ayton

Dog Missing

One gloomy night my mum and I heard our dog barking. We went outside and the stable door was open. We looked all around. We did not find him. We went in the car and shouted. We could hear a voice, 'You will never get your dog back!'

Lucy Fletcher (11)
Roseberry CP School, Great Ayton

116

The Light

I was sitting outside on a dark, cold, misty night. And out of the thick darkness came a glistening light. It was enlarging every second until everything was a silhouette. *Bang!* and the light had landed.

Owen Lyons (10)
Roseberry CP School, Great Ayton

The Great Fire Of London

The bakery was deserted. A light shone in the corner of the room. Suddenly the bakery set alight, all the other houses around it caught fire and kept on going like a set of dominoes. Because the alleys were narrow more than half of London was destroyed in 1866.

Kaitlin Stokeld (11)
Roseberry CP School, Great Ayton

Mysterious Monster

Marty opened three coloured glasses. They were scarlet, chrome, also crimson crystal glasses and they spiralled open, round and round. Suddenly an inconvenient smell met his warty nose. 'Marty, you can't leave goose livers year on end,' he told himself. The stench crept into the jugs. *Bang!* A monster!

Dan Hodgson (9)
Roseberry CP School, Great Ayton

119

Are You Crackers?

The shed door creaked open. Ali was scared. As her grandad said, 'Be careful, nobody's been in that shed since 1994!' In the shed stood a table filled with packets of crackers! The crackers read '2009'. *That's weird,* she thought. Ali then heard footsteps coming up the drive towards her ...

Emma Jane Triptree (10)
Roseberry CP School, Great Ayton

In The Air

It was finally my turn. I put the safety belt on.
Then suddenly I was in the air. I thought I was
going to fall but surely that couldn't happen, or
could it? The rope started to snap but the people
didn't notice. 'Help!' I called out!

Tia Ellahi (11)
Roseberry CP School, Great Ayton

Rapunzel

Rapunzel was leaning out the tower, trying to escape, when she fell out the window. *Oh no*, she thought. She broke her arms and legs. She rolled into the village, her dress was dirty. Then a car hit her and she died. Then the man got out and ran away.

Hannah Tait (10)
Roseberry CP School, Great Ayton

The Sky Glider

The golden eagle soars gracefully through the sky, singing with its magnificent voice. The people below listen and watch with amazement when suddenly, the eagle seeks a mouse, running along the rocks of the waterfall. The glistening silhouette swoops down and aims its sharp claws at the squealing target mouse.

Jodie Vaughan (10)
Roseberry CP School, Great Ayton

Trapped

We were trapped! Stuck in the desert with no food, no water. We were stuck, me and my two friends. Suddenly a giant shadow emerged. What was it? I was petrified. It was a camel. What a relief. A human as well. We were saved at last.

Amy Finch (10)
Roseberry CP School, Great Ayton

Laboratory

A smelly laboratory stood tall. Me and my
assistant, Gordon, were inside making our
new potion. One ingredient remained - *frogs!* I
dropped them in. Put the pan on. *Bubble, bubble*.
Minutes later it was done. Gordon sipped it and
dropped to the floor. Blue steam cascaded out of
his mouth.

Rebecca Storey (11)
Roseberry CP School, Great Ayton

125

Professor Mad

I was all alone in my lab. It was late! I carefully poured the fizzy green liquid into the container followed by the purple. Was this a revolutionary discovery? My blood ran cold as I poured the final ingredient in … *Bang!*

Yazdan Qafouri (10)
Roseberry CP School, Great Ayton

The Car Journey

The summer came, the heat was all too much for me. We got going, it's so uncomfortable with your bags on your lap. It's just horrible. Finally we got out of the car to a fabulous sight of a pyramid. We rented out a camel and rode around the pyramids.

Joe Thomas (10)
Roseberry CP School, Great Ayton

Silence

I was in Germany. Me, Private Miller, my sergeant
and the rest of the squad were held up by an
enemy machine gun. There were only six of us
including me. Suddenly the firing stopped. *Bang!*
The building exploded and then it all fell silent.

Luke Banfield (11)
Roseberry CP School, Great Ayton

Evil Monster?

From the sky, the spaceship hovered down. Who was in it? Nobody knew, all we could do was wait. *Bang!* The door crashed open. A strange-looking creature came out with a reaper's sword and a very dark cape. 'I am the Grim Reaper, let's be friends!' it insisted.

Simon Watson (10)
Roseberry CP School, Great Ayton

The Nightmare

'Hello?' I called out. My voice carried down the empty corridor. My heart pounded in my ribcage. 'Anyone there?' I was terrified.
Someone was whispering, 'Lyla, Lyla.'
I screamed, 'Leave me alone!' My eyes snapped open. It was just a dream.

Bronwen Edwards (10)
Roseberry CP School, Great Ayton

The Curse

They'd finally found it. They slowly entered the
Egyptian tomb. In it was a fortune of gold, enough
for a hundred kings. James didn't hesitate to stuff
his pockets with treasure. Then he dropped
down … dead. With a roar, a huge dog-headed
monster appeared, ran at Daniel and …

Noah Roberts (11)
Roseberry CP School, Great Ayton

A Strange Encounter

4am. I had been searching all night. And on my birthday too. Honestly, I didn't even think aliens existed. But my boss had seen the ship. Suddenly, I heard a strange rustle, and I was being dragged backwards by something into a dark cave. It was a Mercurian Caragnok.

Rachel Harvie (10)
Roseberry CP School, Great Ayton

132

The Thing

I had been searching for aliens all night, when I heard a strange sound. Suddenly I was dragged into a bush. I turned round, there was nothing. *That's strange* I thought to myself. The sound was getting louder. Then I saw a light shine upon me, I ran inside, scared.

George Marsden (10)
Roseberry CP School, Great Ayton

The Graveyard

A heavy storm surrounded us as we took a shortcut through a graveyard. Fear swarmed around us like bats in a cave. Suddenly a figure of clear silk hung above us, screaming an ear-piercing scream, and chased us into a church. The doors slammed behind us.

Gabrielle Margerison (10)
St Joseph's RC Primary School, Chorley

Deadly Mansion

It was a dark, cold night. Four friends moved into a creepy old mansion, not knowing that a zombie was living in the basement. Suddenly a piercing scream was heard. Everyone stopped and looked at a bloodsucking zombie. It chased them around the mansion. Unfortunately it grabbed and ate Gabby.

Niamh McGuigan (10)
St Joseph's RC Primary School, Chorley

Terrible Beast

'You'll never see one,' snorted Jim to Sarah.
She showed him her monster book. 'Yes I will,'
grunted Sarah back, 'there's no doubt I'll find
monsters!'
Jim suddenly felt mottled breath on his neck. His
spine shivered. Suddenly he pivoted round - a
beast glared at him.
'Told you!' giggled Sarah.

Lewis Thompson (11)
St Raphael's Catholic Primary School, Millbrook

136

Mystery

I was walking home when suddenly a bush started moving. I remembered my mum wanted me home by nine, it was now half-past! I looked at the bush again; red eyes peered out. I walked closer, the bush didn't move. I went to touch it and it grabbed me.

Connor Penston (11)
St Raphael's Catholic Primary School, Millbrook

Midnight Surprise!

Creak! Jared woke from his sleep. Looking and listening, Jared cautiously stepped out of his bed. There was another noise. It seemed different this time, it sounded deeper. Jared inched his way to the loft steps. Cautiously he plodded upstairs. Trembling, Jared investigated the room.
'Dad, you scared me silly!'

Jake Chadwick (11)
St Raphael's Catholic Primary School, Millbrook

138

The Mysterious Speeding Stranger

Knowingly, birds crowded overhead. Speedily coming down, the menacing, dying, dim-lit sky. Suddenly the moon stared at the figure descending into a row of monstrous trees. This wasn't the boy's town! But the boy walked down through an alleyway! What was happening? There stood a death-defying door ...

Calum Berry (11)
St Raphael's Catholic Primary School, Millbrook

Shipwrecked!

Mockingly the beautiful bright blue sky laughed at the disgraceful wreck beneath it. The ship felt hurt, lonely and ... broken. Terribly and meanly, the sea was attacking the wreck with its gigantic, heavy, uncontrollable waves! Petrified, the shipwreck lay on the warm sandy beach, paralysed, not able to move itself.

Nicole Lumley (10)
St Raphael's Catholic Primary School, Millbrook

Nightmare Ship

'Hello?' Darrel's voice echoed around the wreck, reminding her of a horror film. Stepping into the captain's quarters, she noticed a faint whiff of corpse, and an eerie banging from behind a locked door. Without warning, it dawned on her. Darrel's consciousness terrified her as the nightmare became a reality …

Sophie Fairhurst (10)
St Raphael's Catholic Primary School, Millbrook

Shipwrecked!

Shipwrecked! Lady May violently washed up onto the unknown shore of a deserted beach. Where was this place? Where were her occupants? Where was her load of gold? Followed by *bang, bang, rumble, rumble, rumble,* like an elephant stamping vigorously on the ground. How would anyone find this shipwreck?

Andrew Robinson (11)
St Raphael's Catholic Primary School, Millbrook

142

The Crash

I run to the airport, I get on the plane. We eventually set off. I hear the pilot talking. I look out the window, the sky begins to change. The plane begins to fall. I feel my stomach turn. My mind fills with dread, I know what's coming …
crash!

Sam Patterson (9)
Stanhope Barrington School, Stanhope

Monsters!

A monster appeared! Scared everyone. They hid.
The monster went away to discuss his plan. He
wanted to take over the world. Peter wouldn't
let him. They had a fight, it lasted a week. Peter
won! The monster disappeared. The people were
saved. They celebrated. It never came back.

Louise Unsworth (7)

Stanhope Barrington School, Stanhope

The Shut Down Terror

Wow! I can see the moon, it's amazing. Hey, what's this? We're spinning. Whoa! *Bang!* 'To the engines.'

'I can't,' he cried. 'We're going down!' he yelled. We tried as hard as we could to get to the engines but it was almost impossible. I felt sick. Oh no ... *crash!*

Tom Lee (8)
Stanhope Barrington School, Stanhope

The Bleeding Cow

All was quiet. A bang! Everyone ran for cover.
Someone shooting. It was a man with a gun.
A cow on the ground, a wound on its leg. It'd lost
lots of blood. It wasn't going to make it. Oh no!
Not another one.

Jake Collingwood (7)
Stanhope Barrington School, Stanhope

The Bad Cricket Match

Thomas was about to bat, it was scary, there were thousands of people. Two people came straight at him and an enormous eagle came swooping down at him. Then suddenly he woke up to find it was just a dream. He looked up, he saw an eagle flying high …

Adam Young (9)
Stanhope Barrington School, Stanhope

The Big Volcano

I heard a creak. I thought it was a wooden door but then I looked up. It was coming down from the volcano! It was very big and full of lava. It was coming towards me. I was at the bottom but it was too late. I was gone forever.

Amy Pinel (8)
Stanhope Barrington School, Stanhope

Lost In The Jungle

He heard a sound in the distance. He shook
with fear. What was getting closer? It was getting
closer but quieter. He started sweating with fear.
Suddenly a white tiger jumped out behind him! It
stuck its claws out and into the man. They fought.
The tiger won.

Timea Dunnery (8)
Stanhope Barrington School, Stanhope

Train Crash

Looking out the window, I heard a spine-chilling noise. The night was falling. I heard the howling of wolves, the moans of dying people I tried to save but couldn't. *Help, what should I do?* I tore through the carriages. Would I stay here forever? A noise … *help!*

Mollie Adams (8)
Stanhope Barrington School, Stanhope

The Football Match

Suddenly the crowd got very excited. The commentators were shouting, 'Will he go for the victory?' Silence descended. They won two-one. The crowd went wild. It was a very exciting match at St James' Park. It was the best match I have ever seen.

Georgia Wright (9)
Stanhope Barrington School, Stanhope

The Extreme Plant

Suddenly the class went silent. Miss watered the seed. The water was taken away, the plant shot up! They all ran outside. The plant grew. Soon it was as tall as the school. Everyone gasped, 'It's giant.'

Seasons passed. Children left, children came, the plant still standing.

It stood forever.

Sophie Bowman (9)
Stanhope Barrington School, Stanhope

152

The Vampires

There were owls hooting. It was midnight,
everyone was asleep except for Abby. Abby
could hear noises, she was frightened. She crept
downstairs, put on her coat, arrived at a town
called Parliament of Blood. She heard a noise. The
gate opened, the vampires had her trapped! She
vanished.

Olivia Parkin (8)
Stanhope Barrington School, Stanhope

King Caspian

Caspian ran. His dad was big and mean. He
tripped. Badger came and helped him up. He
helped the Narnians kill everybody. Next it was
the king. It was hard to kill him. Finally he killed
him.
Caspian took the throne. They had fireworks that
night. Caspian was king!

George Haynes (8)
Stanhope Barrington School, Stanhope

154

The Mystery Death Of Dr Brown
At
The Manor House

'Which one of you was it?' he asked.
'I'm not a murderer.' The others backed off.
'We need to search the rooms.' The inspector
left. He came back holding a dagger. 'Who owns
this?'
'It was me,' growled the professor, 'but you will
not find Brown's body!'
They never did.

Thomas Williams (8)
Stanhope Barrington School, Stanhope

The Fairies

Suddenly, a bang. all the fairies woke. A monster.
They hid. The monster wanted a fairy, he saw her
running with the diamond. The monster yelled
and caught her. He grabbed the diamond. 'At last
it's mine,' he shouted.
'Abracadabra,' the fairies waved their wands. The
monster was gone forever.

Ellie Gardiner (9)
Stanhope Barrington School, Stanhope

The Alien Attack

Up she went to space. She felt her stomach flip.
The rocket stopped dead! Out she climbed. An
alien came. It attacked. She fell down a hole.
Creatures bit her. She reached to escape. She
reached the rocket, she was free at last! But that's
not true, it was there!

Lauren Lee (8)
Stanhope Barrington School, Stanhope

157

Ghost Story

It crept in during the dead of night, sneaked into the hutch and took them. I woke up and they were gone. I ran after him, he dropped one. I kept running. He was gone. I went home. I was sad. My mum and dad bought me a new one.

William Nattrass (9)
Stanhope Barrington School, Stanhope

Friends

Bang! on the door. He opened it. There stood a monster. He ran and hid. The monster sat on the bed. The boy was scared, he shook! The monster wanted to be friends. The boy came out, they played, they laughed. The monster disappeared. The boy hoped he'd come back.

Jason Humble (8)
Stanhope Barrington School, Stanhope

The Scary Monster

The monster attacked, but it was only a shadow.
The people were hurt. How could it be? They
hid. The monster fought the warrior. It lasted for
days. There was lots of blood. The warrior won.
The town was free forever. The monster was
never seen again.

Morgan Allen (8)
Stanhope Barrington School, Stanhope

The Wrestler

The whistle blows, Jeff punches big. Jeff kicks
big. Jeff's worried. Countdown, 3 … 2 … 1. 'I've
won! Come on, I have never been defeated by
anyone for two years.'
He has got the WWE Championship.

Ryan Mackay (7)
Stanhope Barrington School, Stanhope

My Evil Guinea Pig

I want one. My birthday. I'm going to call you Cookie. Cookie does not like me, he is evil. I take Cookie for a walk. I see a man. Cookie kills him. I go to court.
'Are you guilty?'
'No,' I say. I clutch my chest. I live.

Pippa Smith (8)
Stanhope Barrington School, Stanhope

The Faithful Hound

A ferocious hound guarded a tiny baby as a shaggy
wolf knocked at the forboding palace. The hound
fought. Soon there was blood everywhere. The
happy, huge, heroic hound had won.
Finally the master returned. 'What's this?' he
boomed. 'Argh!' He saw the blood, he then
instantly killed his hound.

Arran Stobart (9)
Stanley Crook Primary School, Stanley Crook

The Zombie Attack

One scorching hot day at the desert, I was boiling hot. Luckily I'd brought some water. Suddenly zombies came out of the sand! They started attacking me with big, thick swords. Luckily I found a bigger sword than them. When they came towards me, *smash!* They were all dead.

Rebecca Moore (9)
Stanley Crook Primary School, Stanley Crook

The Rise Of Palkia

In a horrible, gloomy, dark crater lived a terrifying creature called Palkia … Suddenly a load of scary, evil people came, ready to destroy Palkia's crater! Palkia roared to gain tremendous energy! Immediately Palkia released the energy from its sharp white claw and those bad people (Team Galactic) never came back!

Georgia O'Connor (9)
Stanley Crook Primary School, Stanley Crook

World War Two

It was 1940, the Germans were attacking Russia. Me and my teammates were holding them off. They had been a deadly threat but they were pathetic. However, we were running low on ammo. We shot our bullets, they cut through the stupid enemy's skin. It was bloody. However, we won.

Nathan Hodgson (9)
Stanley Crook Primary School, Stanley Crook

The Sound Of The Grave

One terrifying night, a boy and his dad went
hunting for a deer for supper. Suddenly a
mysterious mist came. Once the mist had gone,
so had the boy. So next time you're in the woods
you may hear the screaming of the lost boy.

Liam Clark (9)
Stanley Crook Primary School, Stanley Crook

Dig, Dig, Dig!

One scorching hot, sweaty day, I was digging the daylights out of myself on a desert island. It took twenty whole hours. I dug and dug, I was exhausted. Just then my shovel went *ting, ting*. Then I put some elbow grease into it and there it was, treasure!

Lewis Clark (9)
Stanley Crook Primary School, Stanley Crook

The Lost Scream

One spooky, dark night there was a scared little girl called Ellie. She was searching for the monster from Hell. She searched all night until … the lost scream.

The next day Dad came out to look for Ellie but … no sign. On that night, the monster from Hell killed Dad.

Jak Hope (8)
Stanley Crook Primary School, Stanley Crook

Quest Of The Swamp Monster

One night all was gloomy and it was a dark night.
A knight was asleep in his bed and he heard a
strange noise. He was angry. Then he ran and ran
until he reached the cave …

Christopher Callaway (8)
Stanley Crook Primary School, Stanley Crook

The Twin Savers

One light day in the woods, there were twins
called Ella and Bella and their brother, Max. Max
was asleep in the tent. The bear grabbed Max
with his deadly claws! Suddenly the twins found
Max, made a trap and the bear got stuck.

Emma Macdonald (8)
Stanley Crook Primary School, Stanley Crook

The Lost Pixies!

One blisteringly hot day, a little girl went to see her pixie friends. All the pixies were playing hide-and-seek. Suddenly there were no pixies in sight. The girl searched for hours till it was dark. She went home. The pixies had all gone to bed.

Shania Klijn (9)
Stanley Crook Primary School, Stanley Crook

Day Of Death

My heart was pounding like a meteor falling from the sky. The atmosphere was terrifying as the bullet skidded across the sky. All the other kids were dead, lost or moved. I tried to stop the gun but the man pressed it before I could stop it. It shot me!

Reece Liddle (9)
Stanley Crook Primary School, Stanley Crook

173

On A Hot Day

One sunny, bright day, I went on a trip. I went on
an extremely scorching hot day in a desert. I set
off at twelve. I took my dog. I gave my mam a
kiss, my brothers wanted a kiss, and Dad.
I was thoroughly tired out. I enjoyed it.

Ryan Robson (8)
Stanley Crook Primary School, Stanley Crook

Evil Rag Doll

There was once a girl called Louise. Her mam
bought her a rag doll but it was not any ordinary
rag doll, it could come alive.
That night Louise woke up and she heard,
'Louise, I'm under your bed and I am going to
chop off your head!'
Swish! She was dead.

Ben Robison (8)
Stanley Crook Primary School, Stanley Crook

The Last Deadly Sea Of Souls

Over 25,000 centuries ago, all of the deadly people came up from the sea. We killed Jason, the leader, so all the rest died because they had his blood.

Reese Brown (8)
Stanley Crook Primary School, Stanley Crook

176

The Haunted Mansion

One extremely dark night, in a terrifying mansion,
I got in my bed. I saw a shadow. Somehow it
looked like something was floating in the air. I
thought a ghost was carrying something.
So the next morning I called Ghost Busters and
the ghosts were gone forever.

Arron Stores (8)
Stanley Crook Primary School, Stanley Crook

Untitled

One dark, gloomy night, a brother and sister
were asleep in their cosy, warm beds. Suddenly
an evil dragon angrily swooped down, grabbing
the little boy. The sister woke up, grabbed her
stone collection and threw it hard at the dragon.
He dropped the little boy and he fell fast asleep.

Chloe Shevels (7)
Stanley Crook Primary School, Stanley Crook

The Mean Girl

Once upon a time there was a very mean girl.
Every time the kids looked at the mean girl they
ran away. But one night the kids went to the
woods. When the mean girl was asleep, the kids
went home. Then a witch grabbed the girl ...

Elise Moore (8)
Stanley Crook Primary School, Stanley Crook

Humpty Dumpty And The Death Of The Zombie Master

On a blisteringly hot day there was a memorial, then time suddenly jumped to 12pm at the end of the universe. It went to 12 o'clock then a time portal appeared. humpty Dumpty sliced the time portal open and Humpty Dumpty saved the day.

Louis Gilligan (8)
Stanley Crook Primary School, Stanley Crook

Torture Of The House!

It was midday and the twins named Ellie and Smellie were on their own. In the crooked house they heard a noise and saw a ghost! Even though they were both eight, they knew that water would kill ghosts. So that's exactly what they did. The water killed the ghosts.

Abby Clark (7)
Stanley Crook Primary School, Stanley Crook

A Little Boy And A Dragon

In a small village there was a little boy. He was a legend. His name was Tom.

One day in Rocky Mountains, China, at twelve midnight, a jet-black dragon attacked the village. The next night the boy aimed his bow and shot the dragon.

Liam Walsh (8)
Stanley Crook Primary School, Stanley Crook

182

Fairy And Bogie

Ella woke up. She was so excited, she was going on a date with her boyfriend, Jake. He had something to tell her. 'Ella, here is my secret. I'm a fairy from Twinkle Land. Does it sound weird?' 'No, because I'm a bogie from the land of Snotper.'

Kennedy Zipfel (9)
Startforth Morritt Primary School, Barnard Castle

Mummies

Once upon a time lived the greatest mummy of
them all. Someone had put a scary curse on his
tomb. Whoever dares to go in will have the tall
mummy haunt them forever.
Mark went into the booby-trapped tomb and
opened the sarcophagus, and was indeed haunted
forever.

Nathan Kirby (10)
Startforth Morritt Primary School, Barnard Castle

The Magic Paintbrush

I saw a sparkly paintbrush. 'Wow!' I breathed. I took it home and painted a long tunnel. I tried to do some smudging, but I fell through the painting. 'What has happened?' I yelled. Suddenly I saw an ugly brown monster! He started to chase me and caught me! *Help!*

Alice Peat (9)
Startforth Morritt Primary School, Barnard Castle

Super Space Footy! Zilogs Vs Bullogs

The team is Nink, Jayo, Harto and me. We are
Zilogs. Bullogs are winning but we keep trying.
Nink passes to Jayo. Oh wait, goal! Half-time, 1-1,
it's very tense. If we win, we win the cup! What's
tha ... ?
I got a ball to head and we *won!*

Lenny McLennan (10)
Startforth Morritt Primary School, Barnard Castle

186

The Four-Legged Monster

Wait, where am I? OK, where was I last … ? Oh
yes, I was with my mum. 'Mum, oh Mum, where
am I?'

Miaow.

'What was that?'

Miaow.

'It's getting closer.

Miaow.

My mum has told me about cats! *Run!*

Katie Knox (10)

Startforth Morritt Primary School, Barnard Castle

187

The Spooky Graveyard

It struck midnight. Dale, Arran and Sam went to play hide-and-seek in the graveyard. They had never done this before. They were always joking on about ghosts. 'Bagsy hiding first!' Yelled Arran. He went to hide. He heard a noise, turned around and there was a headless ghost!

Sasha Wilkes (9)
Startforth Morritt Primary School, Barnard Castle

188

My Adventure

I'm going on an adventure. I'm running through a jungle as fast as I can to stop the big hairy monster that's chasing me. *Bang!* I've just run into a tree. *Argh!* It's got me, oh no. It's not, it's a leaf. The leaf is moving! What is it?

James Barber (9)
Startforth Morritt Primary School, Barnard Castle

Trapped Tinkerbell

Lucy had a cat called Tinkerbell, it was black
and white with sharp, long whiskers. Lucy went
in the garden, Tinkerbell followed. Tinkerbell
liked hiding from Lucy, so while she was eating,
Tinkerbell went through the bushes. Suddenly she
was trapped …

Jasmine Banes (9)
Startforth Morritt Primary School, Barnard Castle

Squiggles' Big Adventure

Squiggles the dog was walking in the secret
woods when he fell through a portal to his
magical world. All of a sudden a shoglog
appeared, it narrowly missed him with its pincers.
Dragon came and burnt the shoglog and it was
time for Squiggles and Dragon to go home.

Peter Atkinson (10)
Startforth Morritt Primary School, Barnard Castle

Headless!

I was just nodding off to sleep when I heard a horrible scream from outside. I went over the road, there was the President, laid down, with a panting wolf stood over him. I ran back to my house, I covered my head and heard the distant scream die off!

Britty Farren (10)
Startforth Morritt Primary School, Barnard Castle

The Diwali Danger

It was Diwali, Gretal Goblin was beginning to go home when she saw a haunted mansion. She got closer and closer, then out jumped a dwarf. 'Don't go there,' it said. She ignored it and went in. Then she saw the evil shadow. The door shut and she was trapped!

Victoria Hanley (9)
Startforth Morritt Primary School, Barnard Castle

Choco Friends

White, Milk and Dark were all friends. They
sat on a shelf every day waiting from someone
to take them. They eventually had enough and
decided to move away. They left the post office
and decided to go in the postbox.
The next day they were melted! Dead! Oh dear.

Evelyn Ridgway (9)
Startforth Morritt Primary School, Barnard Castle

194

Hamster Vs Dragon

Diddy, the hamster, was a secret agent working
for HISS (Hamsters In Secret Society). He got a
message on hamcom saying strange sightings had
been reported around his place. 'On it, Boss!'
He set off when the sky burst into flames! When
it cleared it revealed a glittering dragon … *roar!*

Owen Lewis (10)
Startforth Morritt Primary School, Barnard Castle

195

At The Movies

One night Daniel and his dad went to the movies
and Daniel's dad bought a pepperoni pizza before
they went. They arrived and the action movie
started, but Daniel's dad suddenly did a massive
pump and everybody fainted. They had to call an
ambulance but luckily everybody survived.

Michaela Leslie (10)
Startforth Morritt Primary School, Barnard Castle

Best Birthday Ever

It was my birthday, I was going shopping with my mum and dad. We finally got there. 'I'm going to the bike shop.' Dad said and where he was walking, *bang!* I walked into a sign. *Boing!* Suddenly it was raining pencils!

Kane Wynn-Jones (10)
Startforth Morritt Primary School, Barnard Castle

The Treasure Chest

I swayed across the Caribbean Sea with my parrot on my shoulder. Suddenly there was a gold shining light in my eyes. It was coming from the starboard bow of the ship. So my crew turned right and headed towards the cold shining light. It was a treasure chest.

Adam Rumkee (11)
Thorpepark Primary School, Hull

Treasure

I'm a pirate sailing across the ocean looking for the lucky island where the treasure is buried. A mysterious island appears off the portside. I head apprehensively towards it, looking at the dated map. I locate the treasure, my eye patch and false leg, memories of my last trip.

Luke Phillips (10)
Thorpepark Primary School, Hull

My Dad

My dad is a whaler in the Antarctic Ocean. He hunts whales with harpoons. He puts the blubber into boiling pots. The crew in the crow's nest shouts, 'There she blows.' Everyone gets into action. The crew get their harpoons and throw them at the whale. It dies.

Harry King (10)
Thorpepark Primary School, Hull

Mysterious Monster

I was in the car, alone in the dark, gloomy night. Suddenly I heard a bang about a mile away! At first I thought it was thunder, but I looked out of the front window and I was shocked to see no thunder and lightning. I looked forwards and saw ...

Thomas Howard (9)
Warmingham CE Primary School, Warmingham

Deathly Screams

The room was black, I could hardly see more than two inches in front. I could hear the screams of lost souls, crashes of lightning which lit up the night sky. I walked along the creaky floorboards, they creaked and groaned. Suddenly I felt a gnarled hand grab my neck …

Ben Nelson (11)
Warmingham CE Primary School, Warmingham

The Battle Of Gorn

Dragons swooped and dived, dodging the Orcs' arrows that bombarded them. Sweltering balls of fire were coming back at the Orcs, burning them to ash. Suddenly a large, bony, gnarled creature emerged through the gate. It had mighty, wide-spread wings. It was built to fly and kill …

Mitch Crank (11)
Warmingham CE Primary School, Warmingham

The Secret Robbery!

The moon shone, illuminating over the dark rat-infested alleyway. The rats were all quiet until they were disturbed by two robbers. The robbers crept quietly down the alleyway dodging the glints of light. When they got to the end they spotted the bank for the robbery …

Ollie Holmes (9)
Warmingham CE Primary School, Warmingham

One Mysterious Night

One night, when the moon was at its brightest,
a girl went into the darkest forest in Hollywood.
(Gasp!) 'I thought I heard something.' The
footsteps got louder, louder and louder, then the
whole forest could hear it! Suddenly a mysterious
creature appeared …

Yasmin Harrison (8)
Warmingham CE Primary School, Warmingham

The Forged Diamond!

The diamond twinkled in its glass case. An unknown figure sneaked nearer and nearer until … it was gone! The sun smiled happily down on New York.

'The new model will be here soon!' cried Tracy, the secretary.

The door opened with a creak and a beautiful young woman appeared. 'Hi …'

Kate Olbrich (9)
Warmingham CE Primary School, Warmingham

The Demon Of The Underworld

One scary dark night, when a little boy was
reading, he heard a frightening, massive scream
from under his bed. He quickly curled up into a
ball. He peeped out, only to see black smoke had
covered the air, then he saw loads of frightening
gloop rise up from nowhere …

Joshua Bebbington (8)
Warmingham CE Primary School, Warmingham

Information

We hope you have enjoyed reading this book - and that you will continue to enjoy it in the coming years.

If you like reading and writing, drop us a line or give us a call and we'll send you a free information pack. Alternatively visit our website at www.youngwriters.co.uk

Write to:
Young Writers Information,
Remus House,
Coltsfoot Drive,
Peterborough,
PE2 9JX

Tel: (01733) 890066
Email: youngwriters@forwardpress.co.uk